LIFE IN LAKETON

Chancey

WATCH FOR MORE BOOKS ABOUT LIFE IN LAKETON:

1. Back at You
2. After #8
3. Chancey
4. Wildfire!
5. While I Was Out

LIFE IN LAKETON

Chancey

Shawn L. Bird

Flesch reading ease: 90.2
Flesch-Kincaid grade level: 2.6
Font: Open Dyslexic

Chancey
ISBN 978-1-9990509-3-1 (print)
    978-1-9990509-4-8 (ebook)
© Shawn L. Bird. 2022
Series: Life in Laketon #3

Lintusen Press
PO Box 10019
Salmon Arm, BC V1E 3H9
LintusenPress.ca

Acknowledgements

This book began as a NaNoWriMo (National Novel Writing Month) project back in 2013. Many people have helped by reading and offering feedback to get it ready for publication. I know I've missed some of you, but thanks to Vikki, Noelle, and Kirsten for being helpful beta readers.

If you would like to write a novel, check out NaNoWriMo.org and jump in next November! (Or try Camp NaNo in April or June) You never know where it will lead.

1

"Do we have to leave?" I groaned, staring around my room at the huge stack of stuff I had to somehow get into my suitcase.

My mom came in and dumped the contents of a laundry basket onto the bed. "All vacations end," she said with a sympathetic grin.

I waved my hand at the now immense pile on the bed. "How could all this possibly fit into this little case? It defies the laws of physics."

"If you didn't shop while we're here, it would be less of a problem." Mom sank onto the head of the bed, where the stack was low, and exhaled a deep sigh. "I hate packing, too."

"Can't I just leave these clothes here? I'm not going to wear summer stuff in Calgary. It'll be winter the week after school starts."

Mom laughed. "You'll have outgrown it all by next year. This way you can pass it along to Dana."

Dana was my best friend. She is two sizes smaller than I am. Way to rub it in, Mom. "I could go to school here. You know there's a high school. All those kids working in the stores go there. Why can't I?" Our summer condo would be perfectly fine to live in all year. Several of the other residents did. There was no reason we couldn't, too.

"Our jobs are in Calgary." Mom laughed. "Sorry, Chancey. Summer ends for all of us. However..." She rummaged in her pocket and handed me a flyer. "I saw this at the grocery store this afternoon. You want to go? It can be your seasonal farewell to Laketon."

I studied the mini-flyer. It was a photocopied quarter page with a silhouette of dancers and music notes that announced an all-ages dance at the renovated purple barn that served as community centre for the summer village of Laketon.

"I can go to this? Alone?"

"I don't see why not. You're old enough to stay out of trouble, right? Brian needs to get the boat in, but it'll only take the two of us."

"You're sure?"

"The cashier told me most of the town goes to these dances. Kids to grandparents. Seems safe enough, don't you think?"

"You just want some private time with Brian while I'm kept busy." I raised an eyebrow and tried to wiggle it.

Mom laughed, "Well, there is that. How else are you going to get a little brother or sister?"

"Ew, Mom. Gross." Mom and Brian had been married for five years and had spent the last year in a determined baby-making campaign.

My phone beeped and I glanced down at the text.

"Dana?" her mom guessed.

"Yup."

"Get this stuff put away." She dropped the laundry basket at the door. "Anything you don't want, put in the basket and I'll drop it off at the thrift store on our way out of town."

I read Dana's message and sighed.

Went out with Rick last night. I am in love!

Rick was a grade above us. He had dreamy dark curls and worked out. In the last year, he'd gotten seriously hot.

Mom stood up, "What's the news?"

"Dana is going out with Rick."

"Do I know him?"

I shrugged. "I don't think so."

"Is he nice?"

"I guess. He's really cute."

"Cute is okay, but nice is better. I'm happy for Dana, if she's happy, but remember honey, you don't need a boy in your life to be complete. You are a capable, beautiful, intelligent person. You

11

don't need anyone else to be happy."

"Says the woman who gushes and giggles worse than a kid whenever Brian walks in the room." I tried to keep the tinge of mocking out of my voice.

Mom's eyes twinkled. "All right. That's fair, but it took a horrible first marriage to learn I was strong and able. Those qualities were what attracted Brian. A man who respected my strengths was attractive to me." She smirked and added, "and his biceps were attractive to me, too."

I snorted.

Mom chuckled, "I know you don't believe me, but you'll see. A partner who kindles your fire rather than smothering it makes all the difference."

Another text notification binged.

"You'd better talk to Dana before she freaks out." She left, calling back, "Don't be long. Dinner will be ready in a bit."

We have so much in common! Dana had written. **We went to The Beasleys concert and talked for three hours afterwards at Pizza Pizzazz.**

I fought down a stab of jealousy. The Beasleys were just a local band, but they were cool.

Jealous. I typed back. **Going to a dance tonight**, I added, so I didn't sound completely pathetic.

When do you come home? Can't wait to see you and tell you everything!

We leave tomorrow. Sucks to go back to real life. But it'll be good to see you.

School Monday. Summer went so fast! Right?

13

Did you get your summer romance?

Way to dig it in, Dana, I thought. **Tell
you when I see you!** I added a raised
eyebrow emoticon.

Oooh! Way to torture me!

I laughed and hoped that by the time I
saw Dana I'd actually have a romance to
report. **Dinner now. C U soon!**

I stared at the screen at a duck-face
selfie of Dana in her work uniform. Rick
was behind her, making rabbit ears above
her head. They were a cute couple.

When we'd left for Laketon in June,
Dana had challenged me to find a summer
romance, but the hot days had lulled me
into believing I had time. I had spent the
entire summer in Brian's boat. Mom called
it 'idyllic existence' and 'adventure
everyday.' I called it tedious, but I didn't

14

have the energy to go off by myself. It
wasn't fun without Dana.

Most summers Dana came to Laketon
with us, but this year she'd gotten a
summer job.

Mom and Brian still gushed and mooned
over each other like newlyweds, so I felt
like an extra in my own house. Where was
my romance? I was nearly fifteen!

Meanwhile, there was Dana, working in
Calgary, and now she and Rick were going
out. Dana was getting a romance, and it
could keep going through the school year
since Rick went to our school.

I read through their conversation again.
I was the loser who was last to find
someone who liked her. Even Mom had
beaten me to new romance. But I had one
last chance.

Tonight at the dance, I'd see if I could find adventure, if not a romance.

2

I didn't usually dress up in the hot Laketon summers. No one did. Baggy t-shirts and shorts were the uniform of the entire town. But tonight I was determined to stand out. I needed an outfit that announced that I was up for an adventure.

I dug out a tight black t-shirt dress that barely covered my bum, and after some consideration, slipped into bootie shorts for the sake of modesty.

"We're off to pull up the boat!" Mom called up the stairs.

"Okay!" I called back, thankful I didn't have to hear Mom's opinion on my outfit. She probably wouldn't care, because she was cool that way, but she'd be bound to say something embarrassing.

"Be back by ten!" Mom added.

"Okay!" The dance started at six. I'd have four hours. That was plenty of time for an adventure wasn't it?

I went into Brian and Mom's en-suite bathroom to hunt for her make-up bag. I normally just wore lip gloss, but some dramatic eyes could maybe make me look older, more interesting. I pulled up a 'smoky eye' tutorial on my phone and followed the instructions. After a couple of abortive attempts, I got the hang of layering up the colours with the brush. I lined my eyes in black and applied three coats of mascara. I added some blush and a shimmery pink lip gloss.

I rummaged in Mom's closet for a cute pair of low strappy sandals that would work with the dress and ensure that I would be able to dance. Heels might have been nice, but I had to be realistic. I had to walk to and from the dance, after all.

I slipped on the sandals and stepped back to study myself in the full-length mirror.

The effect was definitely dramatic, even if the eyes weren't quite symmetrical. Most importantly, the girl in the mirror didn't look like me at all.

That was a good thing.

I wondered if the kids I'd seen on the beach would think I was new. With the dramatic eyes, was I mysterious enough in this cross between Goth and actress to find some fun tonight?

In the figure-hugging dress and there was no disguising that I was a woman, that was for sure.

Perhaps it was all a bit much for Laketon? I twisted in the mirror, studying all angles.

No, I decided. Tonight, this mysterious drama was perfect.

This was my last chance for adventure.

I slipped some money in the pouch on the back of my phone and tucked the phone into the strap of my bra.

Ready.

My heart pounded just walking down the condo stairs. It felt like the world was tipping off its axis. Why did it feel like everything was about to change?

I practised walking. I tried shoulders back, but that felt like I was presenting my boobs for inspection, and that was just weird.

I tried a rocking motion in my hips that made my butt swing side to side. That was quite fun. A car-full of teens drove by and someone wolf-whistled loudly, cutting the air. I jumped and followed their laughter down the street. They were going to The Purple Barn, too.

Finally, I imagined a string tied on the very top of my head, tugging my back upwards, the movement elongated my spine, tucked in my pelvis, and lightened my step. Ballet dancer walk. Yes. Very confident.

This was the walk of a girl ready for adventure and romance.

This was the walk of someone who was worth knowing.

I arrived at The Purple Barn certain that I couldn't look any better.

SHAWN L. BIRD

"Hey!" someone called from the steps of The Purple Barn. A tall, sandy brown-haired boy about my age waved.

I looked around, but he seemed to be talking to me.

"You coming in here?"

I inclined my head. *Play it cool,* I thought. Then I added to myself, *but not too cool. Don't be a snob,* so I smiled at the boy and said, "Yes. I am. How much is it?" I already knew it was five dollars for singles and twenty dollars for a family because it said so on the flyer, but I had to say something. I was beside him on the step now.

"Ten bucks," he said, sticking out his hand. "You can pay me."

I raised an eyebrow and glanced over his head at the sign. "It says five."

22

He glanced over his shoulder. "Damn. Caught." He grinned. "Pay Judy over there at the table. Save a dance for me?"

He blinked innocently at me and I laughed. "We'll see." Always better to keep them guessing a bit, isn't that what they always say?

I paid my five dollars, got my hand stamped, and went into the barn. On the stage, a band was settling into place, but they hadn't started playing yet. It felt weird to be at a dance without Dana. At home we did everything together.

She'd challenged me to find fun and adventure this summer, and what a woeful job I'd done of it. *Last chance, Chancey, I* thought to myself. *Make this dance count!*

Around the room people were gathered

23

in groups or pairs, chatting. I helped myself to the glass of punch that my admission included and wondered how long it'd be before someone spiked it.

"Hi," purred a deep voice behind me. "Haven't seen you around here before."

I turned and blinked at the stunning guy standing there. Tall. Dark wavy hair. I swallowed my punch and gave him a smile I hoped didn't look as wobbly as it felt. "I've been around," I shrugged. "You weren't paying attention."

A slow smile broke across my face and his eyes shimmered. "Got a name?"

"Yes," I said, and turned away from him. I took two steps, glanced over my shoulder and said, "Later." I walked— *think like a ballerina*—to the doors and stepped out onto the cool step. The band had started playing and the music masked my quivering breaths. *Be cool. Be cool.*

"Hey," said the boy with the sandy brown hair. "Ready for our dance?" He put out a hand.

"Why not?" I said, grabbing his hand and laughing as we joined the crowd on the dance floor.

"I'm Danny!" he shouted into my ear over the thudding bass. "Nice to meet you!"

"I'm Chancey! Do you live here in Laketon?"

"Yup. All my life." The dance stopped and we panted a bit as we walked over to get a glass of water. "Where are you from?"

"How do you know I'm not from here?"

"You're kidding, right? We all start in

kindergarten together in Laketon. There are only a hundred and fifty kids in the elementary school and fewer in the high school. We know everyone. Are you a mystery?"

"Guess so."

The tall dark guy slid between us.

"Danny, introduce me to this lady of mystery."

Danny's eyes narrowed, as if he was considering his options.

"You don't need to know my name," I said, freeing Danny from the responsibility.

"Sure, I do," the dark guy purred, doing something with his eyes that made them smolder dangerously.

"No," I said, lowering the register of my voice. "You don't." Playing hard to get was more difficult that I'd imagined.

Beside me, Danny coughed.

One side of the dark boy's mouth quirked up. "Well then. I guess you don't need to know my name either, right?"

I rolled my eyes and glanced to Danny. "Do I?"

Danny smirked. "Definitely not." He stuck out his hand, "Another dance?"

But before I could reply, the other boy pushed Danny's hand away. "You had your chance. This dance is mine. Come on, mystery girl." And he pulled me out onto the floor.

He could dance. Like, *really* dance. I had never met a boy who could dance so well. It was swing tune, and he spun me, flipped me, and I whirled from arm to arm as if I were some kind of top. I didn't

27

know the steps, but I didn't need to. I felt like I was on one of those reality shows. As the song ended, he dropped me into a dip and I blinked up at him, dazed and amazed.

People around us were grinning. An old couple applauded.

"Still want to go back to dance with Danny?" he said casually.

"Um." I had no voice. "Water?" I croaked.

He grinned.

He set his hand at my back and steered me past the refreshment table, and out the door, grabbing a couple of water bottles on the way out.

"You should use the cups," I murmured. "Bottles are bad."

"Honey, bottles are neutral. I'm bad."

I laughed, still breathless from the dancing, or maybe from the heat of his hand, or perhaps from the promise in his voice that he was offering an adventure, if not a romance.

"Come to me, mystery girl," he said, pulling me off the deck where other couples were standing, fanning themselves and talking.

3

We burst through the doors. I pulled back a little as he tugged me off the deck. "Where are we going?"

He laughed. "I know some comfortable seating, come on." He stopped at a pick-up, tossed the water bottles in, and crawled over the back. He reached out his hand, "Up."

I set my foot on the bumper and he pulled me into the box, where we collapsed in a heap on an old couch that precisely fit the width under the cab window. "Why do you have a couch in your truck?"

"Usually for the drive-in. It's actually a hide-a-bed," he smirked. "Want to hide?"

He reached his arm around me and pulled me tight against him.

"I don't..." I squirmed a bit, but he pulled me closer.

"Come on, baby. You know you want to."

I reared back and stared at him. "Did you just use the most exhausted cliché in the English language to try to persuade me to make out with you?" I threw my head back and laughed, moving away from him while he was surprised. I wanted an adventure, but this was moving a little too fast.

I glared at him. "I don't even know your name. You don't even know mine."

"Ah, but I know you are poetry in my arms," he purred, pulling me back to him. He kissed me and to my complete shock, I melted. It was a minute or two before I pushed away.

Breathlessly, I rolled my eyes and muttered, "Oh, please."

He grinned, "Don't you mean, 'more please?'"

There was thump on the side of the pick-up behind me. "Problem here?" asked Danny casually. He glanced over his shoulder at a couple of his friends who were standing behind him a little way off. "I think it's time she danced with someone else." He looked at me, "Want to come meet my friends?"

I looked between dancer boy and the other three. They were just regular looking young guys in t-shirts and cut-offs. They didn't seem as dangerous as dancer dude, so I reached for the ledge. "Yeah, I think I do." I scrambled over the back of the truck and jumped down next to Danny.

"Thanks," I murmured to him, as we headed back into the barn.

"No problem. I might not be a fantastic dancer, but I'm not an ass-hole like him." He glared behind him and yelled, "And get out of that truck!"

"Do you know him? I don't think I've seen him before." I glanced over my shoulder, to where dancer guy was watching me. I was sure he would have burned himself in my memory if I'd seen him on the beach.

From the truck box, he lifted a water bottle in an ironic toast to me.

"No, he's not from Laketon, but he comes to the dances now and then." Danny looked at "What do you girls see in him?"

I shrugged and without thinking said, "Sex appeal?"

Danny snorted.

"He's an amazing dancer," I added. That dance had been the most incredibly magical experience of my life.

"You know," Danny said, shaking his head, "that isn't even his truck. It belongs to my brother."

"Is the couch really for the drive-in?"

"Yeah."

"Is it a hide-a-bed?"

"No. Just a regular couch. Look, let me introduce you to some of my friends. There are other people to hang out with here. Safer people. Some of us can even dance a bit."

We showed our stamps as we went

back into the barn. A girl with a riot of blonde curls came up to them. "Who's this, Dan?"

"Delia, meet Chancey from Calgary. Delia, introduce her to the gang, eh? Keep her out of trouble."

I watched him go. "He's a real knight in shining armour, isn't he?"

Delia laughed, as she handed me a cup of punch. "He must like you. Or he's growing up."

"What?"

She watched him weave through the crowd. "He's my little buddy."

I sipped my punch. Still not spiked.

Delia took me to a gathering of girls, and I spent the next couple of hours dancing and laughing with them. I kept expecting to see the dancing guy, but he didn't show up.

At ten minutes to ten o'clock by the clock above the refreshment table, I smiled at everyone and said, "I've got to get home. I promised my mom I'd be back by ten."

"Are you walking?" Delia asked.

I nodded. "Yeah. It's just a few blocks. I'll be fine."

The girls exchanged glances. "You know what?" said Delia. "I feel like a walk. Shall we join her, girls?"

Just like that, I had my own squad.

"You don't need to do this, you know."

"Don't be silly. We haven't seen your dancing admirer for a while, but that doesn't mean he isn't around, looking for opportunities. Danny thinks he's trouble, and while my brother isn't the smartest cookie in the box, he has a pretty good sense for trouble; he's been in enough of it. 'Girls should never leave other girls to become a statistic,' my mom says. We have to look out for one another. Too many bad things happen to us."

"But it's Laketon!"

She snorted, "Small towns aren't as safe as you might think. Trust me, we need to look after one another."

We were already half-way to the condo. "That's nice of you," I said. "I appreciate it."

Not a minute later, we heard the crunch of tires following behind us. "Hey, beautiful!" called the dancing guy from the driver's seat of an old sedan. "Ditch the crew! I'd be happy to take you home!"

"I'm good, thanks," I called over my

shoulder. My heart was pounding again.

"Look, I'm sorry I scared you. I'm not a bad guy."

"Take off, creep," snarled Delia. "She's not interested!"

"But she *is* interested," he said, softly. "Isn't that right, beautiful? She's just a little nervous, but I can take care of that. I'll be gentle."

Delia whipped out her phone and snapped a picture of him. "Marie, get his licence plate."

Another girl went behind the car. In BC, licence plates were on both ends of the car. He was from Alberta, then. Or perhaps just his car was.

"I'll get out and pose, if you prefer?" He leaned his shoulders out the window and turned his head, still driving the car forward too close to them, "This is my better side."

"What are you on?" Delia shouted, reaching her arm out to pull me protectively against her. "Didn't you hear us? Get lost!"

He laughed, "Fine, fine!" pulled his shoulders back through the window, revved the car, and drove off, spitting gravel back at us.

We had reached the condo development.

"This is me," I said, waving an arm at the complex. "Thanks for the escort. I guess I did need it after all."

Delia nodded, "He's cute, but he is *definitely* trouble. Will we see you around?"

"Not until next summer, unfortunately.

I leave tomorrow."

"Too bad. Until then, stay away from creeps!" she said as the girls all waved and headed back to the barn.

I glanced over my shoulder and hustled up the steps of our unit. "I'm home!" I called as the door shut behind me.

A muffled noise that I hoped was a greeting came from upstairs.

The lights were out in the living room, but a strip shone out from under the door of Brian and Mom's room.

"Did you have fun?" Mom called.

"Yeah, some local girls walked me home."

"I'm glad you made some friends."

"Yeah, me too." I wasn't going to tell her why. "I'm going to have a bath. See you in the morning."

Her reply was muffled and choked off with giggles. I didn't want to think what that was about.

I ran a bath and crawled into steaming bubbles. The washcloth was soon black from mascara and eye shadow. I leaned back in the hot suds and thought about the night.

It had been an adventure, and while parts of it had been scary, had I actually been in any danger? Surely, not? What would have happened if I'd kept kissing dancing dude? Was he as good a kisser as he was a dancer? My body tingled as I thought about it.

Next time, I'd kiss first and worry later. Next time, I was going to make a romance as well as an adventure. Next time, I wasn't going to pull back.

41

Dana might have a boyfriend, but she wasn't going to have all the fun this school year.

As I soaked into the hot water, I thought about spinning in dancing guy's arms. Remembering the pressure of his lips on mine made my whole body tingle.

Next time I wasn't going to say no.

Next time, I wasn't going to be afraid.

4

Mom was doing the dishes when I came home from school three weeks later. I tossed my backpack onto the floor and opened the fridge, waiting for her to shout at me for not taking off my shoes.

She didn't.

I poured my milk and went into the pantry for chocolate syrup. I reached past her for the spoon, waiting for her to look at me, to tell me chocolate milk had too much sugar, and that I was going to spoil my supper.

She didn't.

I sat at the table in Brian's spot and studied her as I stirred the syrup into my milk and took the first sip.

Her elbows were sunken in the wash water, but she just stared out the kitchen window.

I took a few more sips of chocolate milk, but the pleasure of breaking a house rule was kind of lost when no one actually noticed it.

"Mom?" I said, finally. "Are you okay?"

She inhaled with a quivering sort of gasp and cleared her throat. "Oh, yes. I'm fine, Chance. How was school?"

"Fine."

"Did you have your audition? How did it go?"

"The audition was last week. I told you, remember?"

"Oh." Her voice was very small. "Right."

"What happened, Mom?"

Her shoulders were heaving.

I finished my milk. "Mom?"

She sniffled and whispered. "There's no baby this month."

"Bummer." I tried to sound deeply saddened. I kind of was. She and Brian had been talking about in vitro fertilization if Mom didn't get pregnant soon. The $10,000 procedure would pay for a really nice car for my sixteenth birthday. I wasn't as keen on a baby in the house as they were. "Did you tell Brian?"

She nodded.

This meant Brian would be late coming home. Brian knew that being at home today was going to mean being drenched by my mother's silent tears. It was just as stressful for him as it was for me to cope with Mom's agony. She would weep, and weep, and weep. After a week or so of weeping, she would get extremely cheerful. I would have to wear ear plugs to bed to avoid the embarrassing thumping coming from their bedroom, and we would all pretend everything was fine for three weeks until she got her period again.

"Will Brian be working late tonight?" I asked, even though I already suspected the answer.

She tightened her lips and nodded.

"Right. So, I...um...promised Dana that I'd come to her house tonight to work on our lines for the play." I glanced over to the stove, in the unlikely event that there was dinner lurking somewhere in or on it.

There were no pots bubbling on the stovetop. There was no light in the oven. No ingredients or delicious smells suggested food was on its way.

"Should I pick my own dinner up on the way?" I asked quietly.

Mom sniffed. "I'm sorry, honey. I'd planned to make a lasagna tonight, but the time got away from me."

Of course, it did.

"That's okay." I rummaged in my bag for my script and pulled my coat back on. "I'll be home around eight, okay?"

She cleared her throat and set a plate into the drying rack, "Yeah. Sure."

I shut the door behind me and breathed with relief at my escape.

My mother was inconsistent in her grief. Sometimes she needed me at her side and made me look at my baby pictures while she wept beside me. Sometimes she wanted to watch horror movies and shouted curses at everyone on

47

the screen. It was not pleasant; however she chose to deal with it.

Washing dishes in super slow motion was new, and maybe the creepiest thing yet. I didn't want to watch her self-destruct. Moms are supposed to be stronger than that.

I walked over to Dana's house. Dana had been my best friend since grade three. It was easy being with her. Dana was also, unfortunately, very attuned to my mother's menstrual cycle. When I got to her house though, there was a strange car in the driveway. I hesitated a moment, but then I tapped lightly on the back door and let myself in.

Dana was being engulfed by a pair of broad shoulders and a shock of black hair. I coughed as the door shut behind me, and

Dana squeaked, pulling away.

I smirked at her, as a blush rose on her face. "Hi, Rick." I said, as I grabbed an apple out of the fruit bowl.

Rick blushed, too. "Um. Yeah. Hi Chance."

"Since when have you two been making out in kitchens?"

"Shh!" Dana hissed, glancing furtively behind her. "My dad will hear you!"

"If your dad doesn't think you're together and you're not making out, he deserves to live in his ignorance."

"Huh?" Rick grunted and wrinkled his brows. "What does that mean?"

I laughed. Rick was stunning to look at with his model good-looks and black curls, but he was never going to be on the honour roll.

Dana rolled her eyes. "What's going on?"

"Another month. Another crushing blow for my mom."

She grimaced. "You should come out with us. We're going to see that new alien movie that everyone is so excited about. You know, the one with Damien Dillon."

Damien Dillon was delish. I looked at Rick. "Don't get any ideas about making out with both of us in the dark theatre."

He immediately blushed scarlet and looked frantically over to Dana. "I wouldn't!" he gasped.

Dana smacked me in the arm with a laugh. "Don't torture the poor boy. She looked thoughtfully at Rick. "Do you know someone who'd like to join us? You know, to keep Chancey company?"

"I don't need a pity date, Dana," I growled.

Rick pulled out his phone. "Yes! I do! This is perfect! I'll call Simon. My mom was mad I'd left him alone on his first night staying with us."

I was immediately intrigued. "Who's Simon?"

Our school was big, but if any available guy was called Simon, I'd have known. I loved the name Simon. I had a major crush on a character called Simon Templar from an old black and white British series called *The Saint* that Brian and I watched when Mom was out for an evening. Simon was suave. Handsome. Intelligent. There was definitely no Simon at Morgan Heights.

Rick shrugged. "He's my cousin. He just moved in with us for a while. He's not in school."

This was getting better and better. I looked at Dana, and asked with my eyes, *had she met him?*

She shrugged. That meant no.

Rick hung up his phone. "He's glad to come. He'll meet us at the theatre."

I wasn't so sure about the concept of a blind date, but there was no way I wanted to be at home, so I texted mom, "CHANGE OF PLANS.

GOING TO MOVIES WITH DANA. BACK 10:00." She'd check her phone when I didn't get back at 8:00, and then she'd cry some more. In the meantime, I'd be snuggled up to Rick's gorgeous cousin. With luck, he'd have a British accent.

5

There was a line at the theatre, and the three of us stood shivering in the cool autumn air, waiting to get inside. I kept looking around. "What does your cousin look like?"

"Like me, sort of" grunted Rick with a shrug.

"What does that mean? Does he have dark hair? A cleft in his chin? Dimples?"

Rick shrugged again. "He's taller than me." The line moved forward. I looked around, but there was no sign of anyone arriving who looked like Rick.

"He won't stand you up," Dana said. "I hear he's desperate to get out of the house."

"Why? Has he been on house arrest?" Dana giggled, but Rick tightened his lips and looked up at the posters as the line finally made it through the doors into the lobby.

"What? Has he been on house arrest?" I asked.

"No." Rick muttered, "of course not." He didn't meet my eyes, though.

"Hey!" snarled a voice from the other side of the room, and a huge kid elbowed his way toward us. He must have weighed close to three hundred pounds, his face was covered with acne, his hair glistened with oil in the fluorescent lights, and he looked seriously mean.

I gave a panicked look over to Dana, whose eyes were also wide.

"Excuse me," the big guy said as he

pushed past us and butted into line with his friends, a few people ahead of us.

I closed my eyes and inhaled with deep relief. When I opened them, I looked at a broad chest. I tilted my head up, way up, and met laughing eyes. They were the most incredible shade of green, like a spring tree in bud.

It was the dancing dude from Laketon.

"Hello there," he said. His voice was low and sultry. It made all the hair on my body stand up. I'd forgotten that chemistry between us. He was the most gorgeous thing I had ever seen. He looked like Clark Kent, all tall and brawny. His dark, wavy hair even had the curl in the middle of his forehead tonight.

I opened my mouth to answer him, but I had no words. I closed it again. Then I opened it, again, and made an incoherent little squeak.

He glanced over at Rick. "Doesn't she talk?"

Rick rolled his eyes.

I tried again, "Yes," I squawked. Now I sounded a bit like a chicken, "Hi Simon." I swallowed and cleared my throat. "I'm Chancey." I tried to smile in a sexy sort of way.

He grinned and wrapped an arm around my shoulder. "Oh, I *sincerely* hope so." He showed not the slightest glimmer of recognition that he had once danced with me in a way that I still dreamed about.

In my jeans and jacket, with nothing more than lip gloss, far from Laketon's Purple Barn, was I so unrecognizable from that night?

I glanced over at Dana and she winked at me, standing behind Rick as he ordered popcorn and drinks.

Simon didn't buy anything. I'd have liked popcorn and a pop, but I didn't want to shake his arm off to stop at the counter. We just followed behind Rick and Dana as they went to find their seats in the theatre. We picked out a spot against the wall in the back row.

The lights went out, and Simon's hand moved from my shoulder to hover above my breast. I stiffened. I wanted to say *Whoa, Dude!* but I stopped myself.

I had decided the next time I had a chance with a cute guy, I was going to be braver. This was even better. I was getting a second chance with dancing dude himself. Simon. I savoured the name.

57

Tonight was the night to stop being the safe, predictable Chancey.

I inhaled and pushed my chest upward toward his hand.

My body was alert, every hair tingling upright as he stretched his fingers to brush across my chest.

I held my breath.

What was I doing? What was it about this guy that put my body on high alert?

I exhaled as the screen filled with the previews.

Simon leaned over nuzzled his nose into my hair, breathing into my ear.

I squirmed away, giggling as the air tickled.

In front of us, someone hissed, "Shhh!"

As the movie started, Simon pulled me closer.

I wasn't going to let him take the lead. I was an adventurer tonight!

I turned to him and in the flickering light from the screen, I saw his eyes gleaming. He was interested in me. Even without the skin-tight dress and dramatic make-up, he wanted to get to know me.

Screw it. I stretched up and kissed his lips.

He made a guttural groan of surprise and kissed me back, wrapping his arms around me.

Wow. Could he kiss!

That brief kiss with him in the back of the truck in Laketon had lit sparks, but I'd never experienced anything like this. When he pushed my lips apart with an insistent tongue, I kissed him back breathlessly. I did not see a single scene of the movie.

As the credits rolled, he pulled me to my feet. "Come on!" he said, and I followed him out of the theatre feeling like I was in a dream. In the lights in the lobby, he looked even more like actor Damien Dillon. He was my own leading man. He was so gorgeous! I felt impossibly lucky, like I'd won some sort of lottery.

He pulled me close to him and we kissed again.

My lips were sore and tender from two hours of this, but I wanted more.

Simon broke away and laughed into my eyes. "You are too awesome, Last Chance!"

"Whose Last Chance? I'm an opportunity!"

He stretched his arm over and squeezed my breast, right in front of the line up for the late show. "Oh, yes you are!" he purred into my ear. "I think we need to make this a habit, don't we?"

My cheeks flamed, but I elbowed him in the ribs playfully. "It's a deal."

I had a boyfriend at last.

Simon laughed again as he manoeuvred us through the doors.

Dana and Rick followed us, holding hands.

Outside, Simon kissed me again, then unwrapped himself from me, and nodded at Rick. "Thanks for the invite. See ya around, Last Chance."

Just like that he was gone. I blinked. It felt like the sun had just gone out.   The crowd around us thinned, and I could see Simon walking down the street.

Dana said, "Does he always come and

go so dramatically?"

Rick shrugged. "He has his own way of doing things. Are you all right, Chancey?"

"Huh?"

He laughed and nudged Dana. "We'd better get her home. She looks like she might fall into a coma or something."

"Har har," I said, trying to drip some sarcasm off my swollen tongue. "I can't help it if Simon likes me."

Rick grunted, "Right."

Dana elbowed him hard in the ribs. "Just take us home."

Rick drove us back to Dana's house. The streetlights were a kaleidoscope of colours. I couldn't focus on anything.

My head was swirling. I had a boyfriend who was the sexiest thing I'd ever seen, and he couldn't keep his hands off me. I felt a surge of warmth rush up my spine, like I was super-charged.

"Come on, Chancey. We're here." Dana poked my arm. "I'll walk you home." She gave Rick a quick kiss through the driver's side window and tugged at my elbow. "Let's go."

I was floating down the road. I couldn't stop smiling through my swollen lips. They were going to be so chapped tomorrow. I didn't care.

"Chancey..." she began.

"Isn't he *gorgeous*?" I said, beaming at her. "I can't believe I'm going out with someone like that! I wonder what kind of car he drives?" I imagined the sporty little Volvo from the old TV show and sighed.

"Chancey, maybe Simon isn't quite who you think he is..."

"Right. Maybe I'm the Queen of England. Did you see him?"

Dana sighed. "Would you like to review the plot of the movie; in case your mom asks?"

I giggled at her practicality. "Yeah. You'd better tell me."

She gave me a quick synopsis. She finished just as we got to my house. The lights were still on.

"Good luck with your mom."

I gave her a quick hug and ran to the front door. I'd never been so happy in my life, and on the other side of the door was my mother, who was probably still crying. I tried to clear my face and opened the door.

6

Mom and Brian were snuggled together on the couch. Brian was watching TV looking over her head which rested on his chest. Her eyes were closed. I wondered if she was asleep.

"Hi, Chancey," he said quietly. "Did you have a nice time?"

I tried to make my face as neutral as possible, "Yes."

Mom opened her eyes. "Ooh, baby. You look flushed. Are you sure you're not coming down with something?"

"No. I just walked home with Dana. It's cold outside."

"Ah." She closed her eyes again and pushed her head into Brian's chest. He patted her shoulder absently, as he watched me.

"What movie did you see?"

"*Dark Side of the Mist*. To be honest, it wasn't very good, but that Damien Dillon is so dreamy it didn't matter." I knew my eyes were glistening. I was thinking about Simon rather than Damien, but they didn't need to know that.

Brian snorted. "If you like that creepy, fake-plastic look."

I scowled at him and he laughed. "Oh, I see. You like dolls?"

"I like him," I said firmly. "I'm going to bed."

Mom opened her eyes again. "Are you sure you're okay?" She struggled to sit up. "Let me feel your forehead."

"I'm fine, Mom," I groaned, but I went to

her, and let her put the back of her hand on my forehead. She would keep nagging if I didn't.

She furrowed her brow thoughtfully. "I don't know. Something isn't quite right." She gazed into my eyes, then glanced over to Brian. "Look at her eyes."

"What?" I said.

"Show Brian your eyes."

I turned to him and widened my lids. "What's wrong with my eyes, Mother?"

"Do they look bright to you?" she said to Brian.

"Hmm." Brian said, in a completely non-committal way.

"Do you think she's on some kind of drug?"

"Mom!" I shrieked. "I am NOT on any drugs! Good grief!"

"Fine, fine." She looked at Brian again, then back to me. "I'm sorry. Something's strange, though. You must be coming down with something. You'd better get into a hot bath and get to bed early."

"That was the plan." I muttered, heading upstairs to my bathroom. I ran the water and imagined Simon here. My face was pink, and my eyes sparkled. Simon brought out the best in me, and why not? He was the perfect guy! I added some bubble bath to the water.

I pulled out my phone and texted to Dana, "THANKS FOR INVITING ME TONIGHT. IT WAS AMAZING!"

She replied, "YOU'RE WELCOME. TALK TOMORROW."

I plunged into the hot bath, bubbles puffing around my chin. I closed my eyes and imagined Simon's eyes laughing into mine. I could almost feel his tongue moving through my mouth.

There was a knock at the door, "Chancey? We're off to bed. Good night!"

It was barely ten o'clock. I was going to need my ear plugs tonight. Mom wasn't wasting any time moving onto the next month's baby project, apparently.

I lowered my head into the water, tuning out the world. When I lifted my head out, I could hear murmuring from Mom and Brian's bedroom.

"Maybe we should consider adoption," Brian was suggesting.

That was brave of him.

I couldn't quite make out Mom's strangled reply, but I could imagine her face.

"No, no, honey!" Brian continued, "Don't cry! Of course, I'm not giving up yet, but you need to start considering other options. This hasn't been going well. Perhaps it's time to look at..." His voice trailed off.

Mom was crying loudly now. Her choking sobs were coming through the wall. I dropped my head back under the water to drown them out.

My phone buzzed on the floor by the tub, and I surfaced to read a message from Rick, "SIMON WANTS YOUR PHONE NUMBER. SHOULD I GIVE IT TO HIM?"

I gave a little hoot and sloshed the water as I lunged to grab the phone. I typed, "YES!!!!!!!" then I leaned back and felt myself glowing. Who said love at first sight didn't exist? Or second sight.

Whatever.

I stepped out of the tub and toweled myself off. I massaged body cream in, imagining Simon's hands. Goose bumps erupted all over my body.

My phone buzzed again, and my heart started to pound. I picked it up and stared at the text from the unfamiliar number. "HEY LAST CHANCE. ADD ME"

My hands shook so hard that I had trouble typing his name into my contacts. I should answer him. What should I say? My heart pounded even harder. I was finding it difficult to breathe.

Through the walls I could hear the springs of Mom and Brian's bed bouncing slowly up and down. I needed to get to my ear plugs right now.

I typed, "DONE." I wanted to type, "I

71

love you!" but thought that might seem a bit pushy. Obviously, he liked me, but there was no point being completely crazy.

The phone buzzed again as I was brushing my teeth. My body tingled all over as I read "UR HAWT. C U AROUND."

He thought I was hot! He couldn't spell, but I could live with that. He had other admirable qualities.

I slipped into my pyjamas and started shaking as I climbed into my bed.

How should I reply? "Thanks" seemed silly. Finally, I typed, "C U" and put my phone under my pillow, damn the fire risk. It kept a little bit of Simon beside me. I closed my eyes, put ear plugs in to block the sounds coming from Mom and Brian's bedroom, and imagined his tongue in my mouth, his hand stroking my body. My whole body quivered as I drifted into dreams.

7

Whenever my cell rang or buzzed over the next few days, I grabbed it and sagged when it wasn't Simon.

Finally, I gave up, and I texted him. "HEY YOU! HOPE YOU'RE HAVING AN AWESOME DAY!" Then I waited, heart pounding, for the little tone that meant his reply had arrived.

Nothing.

Dana saw me staring at my phone. "Don't call him."

"Who?" I said, feigning innocence.

She rolled her eyes. "Don't call him. Don't text him. If he's interested in you, he'll call."

"What if he doesn't know I like him?

What if he's shy?"

"How could he possibly not know that you like him? He spent two hours with his tongue down your throat. If you weren't interested in him, you're a slut."

"Hey!"

"But you DO like him, right? So, you're not."

"Right," I glared at her. "I'm not."

"So, wait patiently. You don't want to be pushy."

I pouted. "I don't want to wait."

"That's obvious."

I sat down in a melodramatic huff. I tried to act as if I were joking, but I wasn't really. I thought about Simon all the time. I remembered the magical dance. I imagined his kisses. I wondered if he liked me as much as I liked him. I wondered why

75

he wasn't texting. I sighed.

My phone rang, and after a glance at the screen I grinned up at Dana. "Ha! It's him!"

His text said, "**HOW CAN MY DAY BE AWESOME WITHOUT YOU IN IT? WANNA GO OUT TONIGHT?**"

I grinned over to Dana. "He wants to take me out."

"You're sure that's what he wants?"

"What else would he want?"

"Sex?" she said bluntly.

"Simon is not after some random hook up. He's not like that!"

"How would you know? Have you had a conversation of more than four sentences yet?"

"You're just jealous."

"I have Rick. Remember?"

"Simon is better than Rick."

Dana laughed. "You don't know enough about Simon to know whether he is or not. But that doesn't matter. When is this date?"

"Tonight."

"That's not a date. That's a booty call." Dana shook her head. "Have some self-respect. Don't go."

"If I don't go, he might not call me again."

"Then he isn't worth going out with today. Don't do it, Chancey."

I scowled at her, and texted back. "WHAT TIME WILL YOU PICK ME UP?"

Dana looked over my shoulder as I hit send. She sighed. "Oh, Chance. I hope he's not just using you."

"Just stop it Dana. You just don't know

how I feel. He's amazing. This is going to be the start of something great."

"I sure hope so." She leaned in and gave me a hug. You deserve good things, Chance. Don't under-estimate yourself."

"What are you talking about?" I said, as my phone buzzed again. I turned away from Dana to read it privately.

"MEET YOU AT THE C-TRAIN STATION AT 11."

I scowled for a moment. He wanted to meet at a light rail transit station at night? That wasn't the safest place or time to be out.

"What did he say?" Dana asked.

I shrugged, not wanting to hear Dana's thoughts about this. "I'm going to go home so I can get ready. See you tomorrow."

At the door, she said, "Don't do anything I wouldn't do." She smiled, but her eyes were wary.

"I'll be fine, Dana. Don't worry."

She waved as I left, but the worried expression in her eyes didn't change.

It was just eight o'clock when I got home.

Mom looked up from a magazine she was reading on the couch. "Hey, honey. Did you have a good day?"

"Yeah."

"Do you have any homework?"

"Yes. I'm going to have a bath and get started on it. I'm really tired tonight." I made my way to my bathroom, fighting down the grin that broke with every thought of Simon. If Mom saw, she would know something was going on.

As I ran the bath water, my heart pounded. I was seeing Simon tonight! The thought of him made me happy all over.

Yes, at the back of my mind I knew it would probably be better if he came to pick me up, maybe at a time when I could introduce him to my mom and Brian, but this was okay. This was an adventure! I was glad to be able to spend time with him, whatever we were doing.

As I lay in the bath, I imagined the kids at school seeing me with Simon. They would be so amazed! There was no one nearly as gorgeous as he was at our school. Well. Maybe Rick was close, but Simon was taller and more muscled. And he could dance. I wondered how often he worked out. I wondered when our next school dance was. It'd be awesome to see everyone's shocked expressions as we danced!

I scrubbed and soaked for half an hour, but I actually did have some homework I needed to get done, so I drained the tub and got to it.

At ten o'clock I heard Mom coming up the stairs. She knocked on my door, and stuck her head in. "Almost done?"

"Yup," I said, shutting my math book. "Just finished. How are you doing?"

She shrugged. "I'm fine. Thanks for asking." She glanced over her shoulder and smiled at Brian.

Uh oh. I was going to need ear plugs again tonight.

"Good night, Hon."

"Night Mom. Night Brian."

They headed off to their bedroom and I turned the radio on my old alarm clock.

Through the wall I could hear Mom

giggle, so I put in my earbuds. I grabbed the novel I was reading and tried to ignore the noises coming from down the hall and working past the music coming through my earbuds and the night talk show on the radio.

Finally, things got quiet.

I looked at my phone. It wasn't quite ten fifteen yet. I scrolled through Simon's messages. There were only three of them, but they made me sigh happily.

He was mysterious and cool, just like a handsome spy in a novel. He had so much sex appeal it made me drool just thinking about him.

And he liked *me*.

When my phone said it was ten thirty, I turned my doorknob slowly and stepped into the hall. The radio still throbbed behind me, now it was a Top Ten countdown show. It masked my steps. I snuck up to Mom and Brian's bedroom door and listened. No sound.

I went back for my wallet and jacket, turned down the music enough that if they woke up, they'd think I'd fallen asleep while masking their sounds of romance. They were used to me doing that sort of thing, and they wouldn't bother to come in to turn it off if they got up in the middle of the night.

I slipped on my shoes, eased open the back door, and set off to the C-train station.

8

It was cool outside, and I pulled up the hood and burrowed my hands into the pockets of my jacket. I walked quickly to try to generate some heat. It was peaceful out.

The windows were all black on my street, except the Davidson's on the corner. They had a new baby and the nursery lamp glowed faintly through the pink curtains. I wondered if someday Simon and I would be up late cuddling a baby in our own nursery. The thought made me smile as I rounded the corner and moved into a jog.

There was a group of guys outside the pub. One called out, "Hiya, babe! Wanna party?"

Another laughed and shouted, "You're not man enough for a pretty lady like that. Come on, sweetie pie. You shouldn't be out here all by yourself. I'll take care of you!"

My heart pounded. I kept looking forward and moved a little faster.

The C-train station was lit up, and there were cameras there, so it was unlikely that there'd be any trouble, but I did wait in front of a camera, just in case. The guys outside the pub were unsettling, because while that guy was undoubtedly drunk, he was right. I *shouldn't* be out here by myself.

"Boo!"

I squealed and my heart exploded out of my chest and into my throat.

Simon laughed, and wrapped his arm

around my shoulders, squeezing tightly as he leaned down to kiss me. "Hey, Last Chance. Ready for an adventure?"

"Sure," I said, when I got my breath back. "What are we doing?"

He grinned. "Train coming!" He led me onto the platform as the train pulled in. "We're going downtown, where the action is."

There was no one on the train when it pulled in.

The protective drunk from outside the pub sauntered up the platform with determined casualness, as if he was trying hard not to show that he was having trouble walking in a straight line. "Is this guy bothering you, sweetie pie?"

"No." I said, looking away from him.

Simon kissed me again, thoroughly.

The drunk coughed. "That's very rude behaviour," he said. "A gentleman should be more respectful of his girl."

Simon's smile spread slowly, and he kissed me again, forcing his tongue deep into my throat. I tried not to gag. It wasn't very romantic making out in a train in front of a drunk. He lifted his head and levelled his gaze at the drunk, daring him to say anything again, but the drunk just shrugged.

"You're sure you're okay with this guy, sweetie pie? He seems a trifle lecherous."

He seemed genuinely concerned, so I smiled at him. "It's okay. Thank you for your concern."

"All right then," he said, moving to the door so he was ready for the next stop. "You have a good night, ya hear? Stay safe!"

"Good night," I replied as he left the train.

"What a loser," Simon said, kissing me again.

I wiggled my head out from under his. "Is it much farther?"

"Here," he said, standing, as he grabbed my hand and pulled me after him. We're getting off here."

At this station, there were actually people on the platform waiting for the train, but again most of them looked inebriated. I wondered if sober people ever came out at this hour. Simon pulled my hand and dragged me down an alley. It smelled of urine and vomit. I pulled back.

"What?" Simon's brows were down.

"It stinks down here! I don't want to go

there."

"It's fine. It doesn't stink inside."

"Promise?"

He grinned, and this time his smile lit his eyes. "You're going to love this."

My stomach jolted at his smile.

He indicated a shiny red door. "It's right here. Come on, Last Chance." He jiggled the door handle, but it was locked.

My heart dropped a little, but he knocked, and it opened a crack. Soulful music oozed out.

"Hey Robin! It's me, Simon. Can my friend and I come in?"

A hairy head poked out of the crack. Little black beetle eyes peered out between long dark wavy hair and a bushy beard that looked like it was heading to his waist. He looked me up and down and grunted. The door opened, and Simon and I ducked under Robin's arm and into what turned out to be some kind of club.

They didn't seem to believe in the non-smoking ordinances, because people were smoking all over the room in deep leather-vinyl booths. Girls carrying small drink trays were wearing tiny skirts and tinier shirts. They didn't worry about ages of the clientele either, since no one seemed at all concerned with us. I don't know, maybe Simon was actually old enough to be here, but I sure wasn't, and it was weird that no one seemed to care.

"A gin and tonic for me," Simon said to a cute little blonde in a pink micro-uniform, "and a Singapore Sling for the lady."

"What's that?" I asked, as the waitress left.

"Girly drink. You'll approve."

"Gin and tonic?"

"Manly drink. I approve." He grinned.

A band made its way onto the stage and settled in. The soulful canned music stopped, a big guy started beating out a rhythm on the drums, and suddenly the club was full of music. Brilliant music. Astonishing music. Music that reached into my brain, dived into my belly, and wallowed around. It made me want to move, it made me want to sing, to dance, to cry, and to sleep all at once. "Oh!" I gasped.

Simon smiled. "Incredible, eh? I thought you'd love them." He wrapped his arm around me, and I nestled under his shoulder, endeavouring to sip my pink drink without stabbing myself with the little umbrella.

There were just five instruments: a baritone saxophone, a soprano saxophone, the drums, a clarinet, and a trumpet. They were winding tunes around themselves and spinning them into the air. This was a mix of jazz, blues, heavy metal, and rock. It was familiar and new. It was simple and complex.

The drink made me feel pleasantly warm and lazy. The music made me feel alive. Simon made me feel electric. Between the three of them, I was enclosed in a bliss that I could never have imagined. I was with a man I loved, having an adventure so wonderful it was almost a dream. Simon met my eyes and kissed me again. My body throbbed in response.

It was nearly three o'clock in the

morning when Simon pulled me to my feet. "Come on, Last Chance. Time for us to get on the homeward journey." He waved to Robin the doorman, and we walked, swinging our hands in a blissful revelry.

"Have fun?" he said, grinning at me.

"Oh, yes. That was fantastic. How did you know about this place?"

He shrugged, "Connections." We walked up to the C-train platform. There were still a few drunks around. I didn't see anyone who was sober, except the security guard who stood by the elevator. His eyes were suspiciously blood shot, though.

The screen announced the next train and Simon let go of my hand. "Thanks for coming out tonight. I'll text you later."

"You're not riding home with me?"

"No, I've got somewhere else to go.

Here's your train. Bye!" He gave me a little shove as the doors opened, and I automatically stepped through them.

"Simon..." I began, but he grinned and spun on his heels, heading for the stairs before I could finish my thought.

The train arrived.

A very smelly man sat at the seat behind me and leaned forward as if he wanted to talk. I opened my phone and opened a book app. While I pretended to read, I scanned the creepy late-night passengers.

How would Simon feel if I was murdered on the ride home? Would he regret just pushing me onto the train and abandoning me?

He had somewhere else to be, though. Maybe he was volunteering at an old folks' home or something,

I didn't meet anyone's eyes as I got off the train, and headed home. There wasn't anyone hanging around outside the pub now.

On my street, even Davidson's nursery light was off. I slipped quietly in the back door and slid the lock bolts home. I took off my shoes and crept quietly into my bedroom. The house was silent.

I set my stinking clothes in the hamper and crawled between my sheets. I was asleep before I could even set the alarm.

9

When Brian woke me up at seven o'clock, I felt like my eyes were glued closed.

"Whoa, he said. "You don't look so good. Are you sick?"

I struggled out of bed, "I have a math test this morning. I'll be fine."

I got to school more or less on time. I wrote my math test, and probably passed. I kept sneaking glances at my phone all morning, wondering if Simon had texted and I'd missed it.

At lunch Dana came and sat with me. "We should probably talk about Simon," she said.

"Isn't he great?" I sighed. "I can't believe we're going out."

"Yeah. About that..."

Rick muscled in between us at that moment, grinning at Dana. "Are you going to help me with that math like you said? You had the test, right? I have it after lunch." Rick had failed math last year and was repeating the course.

Dara glanced over at me, and then shrugged, "Sure. Of course. Right now?"

"Yeah." Rick pulled a folded piece of paper out of his pocket and set them down in front of Dara. "I couldn't figure out the answers to these three questions."

My phone, tucked under my bra strap, started to vibrate. I jumped.

They looked up, confused.

I laughed awkwardly. "I'll talk to you guys later, okay?" I sped out of the room, looking for a private place to answer the phone.

I ended up in the handicapped washroom. No one was likely to be hammering on the door. "Hi!" I said, as I turned the lock on the doorknob.

"Were you avoiding me?" laughed Simon.

"I had to get somewhere private. I didn't want anyone listening." I sat down on the toilet, fully clothed.

"Wise of you." He chuckled in a rumbling bass that had my belly flopping like a fish was trapped inside it. "Where did you end up? I hope you're not stuck in a reeking janitor's closet or something?"

I laughed. "No. A nice little room with a lock, that's all." I double checked the lock was engaged.

"Look, I've heard word of a special

event tonight. I think you should come with me."

"I..." I had a rehearsal for community theatre tonight, but I would skip it to be with Simon. "I'd love to come. What time?"

"I don't know yet. I'll call when I know, okay?"

"Yeah. Sure. I'll be ready."

"I'm looking forward to being with you again, Last Chance." His seductive purr told me how much.

"Me, too. I mean, seeing you." My heart was pounding so hard, it was hard to hear him. "See you tonight." I put the phone in my pocket. I was having difficulty breathing again. I looked into the weirdly slanting mirror, set for viewing from a wheelchair. If my mom could see my eyes right now, she'd be sure I was high.

I was high! I was high on Simon! I was so lucky to have a boyfriend who made me feel like this!

Dana was in the hall when I came out of the bathroom. "Why were you using that one?" she asked, brows down.

I shrugged, "I was in a hurry."

She shook her head, "We need to discuss that guy, you know."

"Who?" I didn't know what she was so intent on saying, but I didn't need anyone bad mouthing Simon. I knew he was perfect for me.

She rolled her eyes. The bell rang at that moment and cut her off. "I'll meet you at your place to go to rehearsal tonight, okay?"

"Oh. No. Not this week. I have a meeting to go to."

"Meeting?" she said, suspiciously, "Who are you meeting? You know that we're supposed to be working on that really tricky combination leading up to your solo part, right?"

"Yeah, but I really have to go to this meeting."

The vice-principal cleared her throat behind us. "Ladies? Don't you have some place to be?"

"Yes, ma'am!" We said in unison and headed to our classes in opposite directions.

I snuck out a back entry after school so that I wouldn't run into Dana. I raced home to change into clothes for 'something special.' A dress this time. I waited for Simon's call. Then I changed again, this time into jeans. Then I changed a third time in a skirt and cropped shirt. I wanted the perfect mix of sexy and... well...sexier.

Mom's car pulled into the driveway just as I had settled on my fourth outfit: skinny jeans, a black bra and a sheer white boyfriend shirt. I took off the shirt and put on one of Brian's hoodies for now.

My phone buzzed and I leapt across the bed to check the text, but it was from Dana, "YOU SURE YOU'RE NOT COMING?"

I scowled at the phone.

Another text buzzed in, "PATTY IS GOING 2 B FURIOUS IF YOU MISS PRACTICING YOUR SOLO."

"SORRY. MEETING. C U TOMORROW." I hit send with a purposeful whack of the key. So there.

Her reply popped back almost

instantly. "IF YOU'RE MEETING SIMON, DON'T. IT'S NOT WORTH IT."

I stared at the phone with my mouth agape. Simon not worth it? It wasn't worth missing a rehearsal to be with him? Was she crazy? Simon was everything I'd ever dreamed of in a boyfriend. Of course, there would be sacrifices to be with him, but I would pay them. He was absolutely perfect. I would never have thought Dana would be the jealous type.

"Chancey! Dinner!" Mom shouted.

I adjusted the hoodie over my hips and headed into the dining room. It smelled really good. Brian came in from the family room and did a double take. "You're wearing my hoodie?"

"Yeah. It was in my clean clothes basket. Jeanne must have put it there."

Jeanne was the housekeeper. "Did she make dinner?"

Mom nodded, "Jeanne is a gem. What would we do without her to keep the house in order?" Mom set a steaming lasagna on the table and went back for the Caesar salad.

As she set it down, Brian raised an eyebrow and the salad tongs, "Other people manage to look after their own house full of kids, Meg. It's not like you're working all day." He chuckled as he put the salad on his plate and passed the bowl to me. Garlic wafted up from the Romaine lettuce.

Mom pouted in a cutesy sort of way, like she was just pretending, but then she started blinking back tears. She sniffed and looked away.

"I'm sorry, hon." Brian said, as he pushed his chair away from the table and wrapped his arms around her, rocking her gently back and forth. "I'm sorry. That was inconsiderate of me."

She shook her head and cried. I cut a square of lasagna and started to eat, ignoring them as they stood beside the table, arms around each other, rocking. Tears dripped off Mom's chin.

I chewed.

Mom sniffed, "Don't you have rehearsal tonight, Chance?"

The phone buzzed in my bra. I jolted. "Oh! No! No rehearsal! I'm feeling sick! I bulged my cheeks and pushed back my chair. I raced into the bathroom and leaned against the door while I dug under the hoodie for the phone.

I pulled it out to read, "LAST CHANCE..." my heart did a flip, until I noticed the rest of the message, "...FOR A RIDE TO REHEARSAL." It was only a message from Dana.

Where was Simon's text? Maybe he was dialing the wrong number. Maybe something had happened to him.

I could hear someone in the hall, so I made gagging sounds, then flushed the toilet with a melodramatic groan.

"Are you okay, Chance?" Brian asked.

"No," I said weakly. "I'm going to bed." I kept my eyes down and shut my bedroom door firmly behind me.

10

I lay on top of the bed in my clothes. I looked at the clock beside my bed. Seven o'clock.

Why hadn't Simon called yet?

Was he hurt?

Had he been in a car accident this afternoon?

I stared at the ceiling, worrying.

An hour later, my phone buzzed, I grabbed at it, but it was just Dana again. "PATTY IS MAD."

Who cared? Simon was lying in a ditch somewhere.

I crawled under the covers, my heart aching. What had happened?

My phone buzzing woke me up. I

grabbed it and read, "READY?"

I blinked, what was Dana trying to tell me now?

Then I blinked and read the message again. It wasn't from Dana. It was from Simon.

Was I ready?

I sat up in bed, typed, "YES" and flipped the covers back as I checked the time. Midnight.

The house was dark and silent. I had to pee but didn't want to wake them with the flush. The phone buzzed again. "MEET YOU AT CROSSROADS CAFE IN 15 MINS."

I gulped. How would I get there? It was only five minutes to drive there, but unless I jogged, there was no way I'd get there in fifteen minutes. I didn't want to risk having him change his mind.

"**Sure**," I wrote. For Simon, I would run.

I grabbed my coat and crept down the hall. The back door had two dead bolts. I tied my boots, and then slipped the bolts back as quietly as I could. I held my breath, straining to hear if there was any stirring upstairs. I eased the door open and slipped outside.

It was cold. I started jogging down the road. I checked my phone. Ten minutes to go. I was not quite half-way there. I didn't want to arrive looking sweaty and red-faced, but I didn't want to be late, either.

I slowed and looked around. The streets were completely empty. I started jogging again.

When I got to the café, the lights were on, but no one was inside. I pushed in the door and headed right to the bathroom.

When I came out, a waitress was behind the counter. "Hi," she said, "can I get you something?"

I sat down at the counter in front of her, "Yeah, sure. Can I have a coffee? Double double."

She nodded and grabbed the coffee pot and a mug. "We have good muffins. Only a dollar."

"No, thanks. This is fine."

She shrugged and went back into the kitchen. I sipped the coffee and wondered what had happened to Simon. Had he been hit by a car? Had he been mugged?

I was just about finished my coffee when the bell on the door tinkled. "Hey, Last Chance."

My face split into a relieved grin. "Hi!"

"Ready to go?"

I swallowed the last of my coffee. "Where are we going?"

He wrapped his arm around my shoulders. "Party. You'll have fun. Come on."

I tossed a twonie onto the counter, and called out, "Thanks!"

The waitress said something that I didn't catch, and Simon and I headed into the night.

I looked around for Simon's car, but the lot was empty. "Where is it?"

"Not far, come on." He slid his hand down my arm and grabbed my hand. "Let's go!" He started running, dragging me along behind him.

I laughed, stumbling to keep up in my boots. "Slow down! What's the rush?"

He stopped suddenly. "You're right.

What am I thinking?" He curled me into his chest and kissed me.

He smelled so good. His skin was spicy and smoky like he'd been sitting around a campfire. My head swam, as he pulled his lips off my mouth. "Mmm. Chance, you are a lucky charm. Come on." He tugged me along, and I kept step. His legs were so long that to match his pace, I had to take two steps for every one of his. He squeezed my shoulders. "You are so adorable. Here it is, come in."

The house was kind of creepy. The siding was dark. There was a front porch, but it was missing pieces. The door was scratched up. The streetlight above us wasn't lit, so we were standing in a hole of darkness. I could feel the throb of music coming from inside. No light leaked through any of the windows.

"There's a party here?"

"It's a private party. There aren't many people here, but don't worry. You'll be fine." He smiled down at me. In the light from the streetlight further down the street, his eyes were glowing, and when he kissed me again any doubts I had melted right away. When we came up for air I blinked.

He grinned, "You are damn sexy, kid."

I stuck out my bottom lip and blinked up at him in what I hoped was a sexy way. "I'm not a kid."

He raised an eyebrow.

"How old are you, Simon?"

He laughed and gave my shoulders a squeeze. "Old enough to know better and young enough to do it again. Let's go in."

He opened the battered door, and we went inside.

11

It was dim. Simon guided me down the hall and then opened an interior door. "Watch your step on the stairs."

I reached for a railing, grabbed it tightly, and stepped into darkness. There was a strange smell, kind of like incense. I stumbled a bit when I got to the bottom, reaching for another stair step and meeting the floor instead.

Simon grabbed my elbow. "Are you okay?"

"Yeah," I whispered. My heart was thundering. This black space was so weird, but in a cool way, of course.

Simon whispered in my ear, "Prepare for your doooooom! Mwa ha ha!"

He guided me around a corner where an eerie glow showed beneath a door. Simon pushed it open to reveal six guys, sprawled on chairs, couches and the floors, game controllers in their hands, all staring at a huge big-screen TV. Other people were in corners around the room.

"Hey," said Simon.

"Shut the door."

He shut the door, "I brought a friend. Ethan, give her your chair."

A lump curled in a recliner grunted. "I was here first. Besides, I'm about to kill the dragon. I can't...arg!" On the screen, a tiny knight was devoured by a glittering scarlet dragon. "Women are bad luck in the gaming room!" He glared at me.

Simon laughed. "She's here to be my good luck charm. Shove over.' He squeezed onto a couch, reaching for a game controller with one hand, and pulled me down onto his lap with the other.

A haze of dry ice was drifting up from one corner and the blinking of a strobe light cast a surreal spell, like a haunted house. There were several couples in various corners of the room standing at a bar, curled on couches, and draped over each other on oversized floor pillows. A hypnotic rhythm was echoing around the space. It pounded into my brain.

Simon squeezed my hand and pulled me up against him. He moved to the throbbing rhythm, and I moved with him.

Someone else came up beside us in the flashing darkness and whispered to Simon. He laughed and pushed me into other arms. I couldn't really see his face. He rubbed up and down on me as we danced. It was gross. I twisted my head to look for Simon. Between the flashes, I finally spotted him over at the bar.

In choppy movements like a silent movie, he approached and shouldered between me and my partner. He handed me a bottle, "Have a drink." I read his lips since I couldn't hear anything but the throbbing music. Perhaps he said, "This is pink."

"What is it?" I shouted over the music.

"What?" he yelled back.

"WHAT IS IT?"

He shrugged and pointed to his ear. He smiled and took a sip.

I shrugged back and tried it. It was sweet and fruity. I smiled and took a bigger swallow.

He dragged me over to an empty couch and pulled me down. He tilted his glass and chugged the whole thing down. I followed his lead. When my glass was empty, he took it from my hand, and leaned over and started kissing me. He started at my hand, and kissed all the way up the arm, all around the neck, and then down my chest and over onto my belly button. I pushed him off, giggling. Grinning, he came down to my mouth and we began kissing in earnest.

His mouth tasted of fruit: strawberry, grapes, peach, and pear.

His hands were everywhere, cupping under my butt, rubbing up and down my thighs, curling around my breasts. My body was on fire.

Then there was a vibration in my bra

that jolted me.

My phone.

It was probably Dana.

I ignored it.

Simon's body was up against mine, and we were both panting slightly.

My phone buzzed again. "Damn it!"

I pulled slightly away from Simon and checked the screen. "YOUR MOTHER DOESN'T KNOW YOU'VE SNUCK OUT, BUT SHE WILL IF YOU'RE NOT BACK HERE IN 10 MINUTES."

"Oh no!" I struggled to stand.

Simon's lips formed, "What?"

I passed him the phone to read the text. "It's my step-dad!"

He gave me a twisted smile and shrugged, leaning back.

I took my phone back and frantically typed, "I NEED 20. I'M COMING. DON'T TELL!" I tugged on Simon's arm. "I need to go! Help me find my way out of here!"

He rolled his eyes but stood to lead me across the floor.

Somehow, he found the door, and we made our way up the stairs and outside. The irregular streetlights seemed dazzling after the surreal effect of the strobe.

"I'm sorry. I have to get home or I'm going to be in serious trouble."

He didn't say anything, but we set off, jogging down the road. I felt dizzy, and I wondered again what the drink had been. We got to the café and he stopped, puffing. "Right. You know the way from here, yeah?"

"You're not taking me all the way home? What if there are rapists and muggers out? It's after two in the morning!"

He laughed and kissed me quickly. "Talk to you later," he said in that low, sultry voice that made my spine melt.

"Yeah," I drawled, my brain processing in slow motion after the kiss. "Okay."

He turned around, heading back to the party, and I began to jog home. I made it in nineteen minutes from Brian's text.

The light was on in the kitchen.

I opened the back door quietly and stepped inside.

Brian was sitting at the kitchen table with a mug in his hand. He met my eyes and studied me. "Hot chocolate?" My favourite mug was already at my regular place at the table.

I sat down.

Brian studied me. Finally he shook his

head. "Why don't I think you were out with Dana?"

I shrugged and sipped the hot chocolate. It was good, better than when Mom made it. Brian was very good at comfort foods.

"Oh. I know," he answered himself. "Because Dana is sensible and respects the basic concepts of safety and security."

I shrugged again. Dana was not as perfect as he thought, but I wasn't going to get her in trouble, too.

"So, where were you?"

"At a house," I said, keeping my eyes on my mug.

"With?"

I sighed. "My boyfriend."

"Oh? Does this boyfriend have a name?"

"Simon."

"Like The Saint?" he said, and he laughed.

I couldn't help grinning. "Yeah. And he's just as handsome as The Saint."

"But he doesn't have the cool car, I take it? It looks like you've been running."

"Yeah. Well. I was in a hurry you know."

"You know that guys who want you to sneak out are not the kind of guys you should be going out with, right?"

I sighed. "That's what Dana says. But honestly, Simon is fun. He knows all these great places. He's Rick's cousin. It's fine. I promise."

I set down my empty mug and stood up. "Thanks for the hot chocolate."

"Chancey. It's not safe for you to go out like that. If something happened, we'd have no idea where to find you. Don't do it again, okay?"

I shrugged. If I was going to keep seeing Simon, and obviously I was, then I would probably have to go out late again.

"I'm serious." Brian leaned closer, holding my gaze. "If you don't want your mom to know, text me. But I'd rather you didn't sneak out at all. Any guy who wants you to sneak out to see him isn't showing you the kind of respect you deserve. I don't know your Simon, but so far I'm not impressed."

"Brian..."

He held up a hand. "I'm not arguing with you at this hour. I'm entitled to my opinion, and you're entitled to a boyfriend who respects you. And you're grounded next week. You're going to decline all invitations and stay home watching TV with us or catching up on your reading. Is that understood?"

I sighed and nodded.

He stepped forward, pulled me to my feet, and gave me a hug. "Go to bed. You're getting up in five hours. Sleep well."

"Good night, Brian. Thanks for keeping this between us."

"For now. I expect you to tell your mother about this young man sooner rather than later. Good night, Chancey."

I turned around at my bedroom door, and he was still in the kitchen, holding his mug, staring at the table.

12

"Come on, Chancey." Dana wheedled. "It's my birthday! You have to sleep over!"

"I don't think I can. Brian knows about Simon, but I'm not ready to tell Mom yet. I promised I'd stay home this week."

Dana pursed her mouth and fluttered big, sad eyes at me. "Please come? It'll just be the two of us. Like the old days. Rick is taking me horseback riding on Saturday, but I want to celebrate with you on the day. My parents have to go see Aunt Edie. I don't want to be by myself on my birthday!"

"I'll ask Brian. It'd be fun to sleep over. It's been a while"

To my surprise, Brian didn't mind. I think Mom had told him she was planning a romantic evening, and they were happy to have me out of the house so they could run around naked and have sex on the kitchen table, or whatever it was they did on their romantic weekends. I didn't ask them for particulars.

Brian studied my overnight bag and met my eyes. "Stay out of trouble, eh?" His meaning was clear.

"Of course. Dana has planned dangerous things like painting our toenails and giving ourselves mud facials."

Mom laughed, "Chancey always stays out of trouble, don't you?"

Brian raised an eyebrow that only I could see, but he didn't say anything.

I walked directly to Dana's house, but

128

sleeping over there didn't mean I didn't have my own opportunity for romance.

When Dana's back gate shut behind me, I sat on her porch chair to send a text to Simon. "**Sleep over at Dana's tonight. You and Rick want to come?**"

"**Hell, ya!**" he wrote back immediately.

I met Dana at the door with a huge grin across my face. "Guess what?" I shrugged out of my pack and dumped it on the tiles at the back door.

"What?" she asked warily.

"The guys are coming over."

She scowled. "I'm making pizza, and I've downloaded some movies for us. I thought we'd watch some feel-good chick flicks. Girls' night. You know?"

"You're making pizza from scratch?" I shook my head. "You amaze me."

"You're helping. I made the dough this morning, so it is ready to go." She sighed. "The guys aren't going to want to watch my chick flicks."

I shrugged.

"Whatever," she said. "Come on."

She dragged me into the kitchen and wrapped a frilly apron around my waist.

I looked like a French maid. "Are you serious? What is this supposed to protect my clothes from?"

"Who cares. What are the guys going to watch?"

I shrugged. "They'll just download something. No biggie."

She sighed again as the doorbell rang. "I was really looking forward to watching some movies where nothing is shot or explodes for my birthday."

I grinned. "Sorry."

"You just grate that cheese."

I grated while she went to the door to let Rick and Simon in. I focused on my task, but arms wrapped around me from behind and lips kissed my neck. "I love the apron," Simon whispered into my ear. "Very sexy."

I batted him with the grater. "Silly. It's supposed to keep my clothes clean."

"Mmm," he said, nuzzling my neck. "Right."

"Come on, you two," said Dana. "Help make these pizzas. Rick, here's the dough, do you want to roll it or throw it?"

Rick's eyes twinkled, as he grabbed the dough, "Throw!"

I expected we'd be pulling clumps of dough off the ceiling, but to my surprise,

Rick was actually pretty good at tossing the dough into the air, spinning it so that it spread until it was a nice sized disk.

"How did you do that?" I demanded.

He laughed, "Summer job at Luigi's. The ladies love watching a handsome young man like myself tossing a pie."

Dana fluttered her eyes at him and tossed him another ball of dough, "Oh, *signore*," she said in a fake Italian accent, "do it again!"

He kissed the finger-tips of one hand while he spun the dough up with the other one.

Simon pulled a knife out of the block and set it on a cutting board. He reached out to Dana, "Salami if you please? I can slice as well as he can toss."

I imitated Dana's blinking innocence,

"Oh, kind sir, do be careful with that big salami!"

Simon threw back his head and howled with laughter. "Oh baby, never fear, there is salami enough for you!"

Dana rolled her eyes, but Rick and I laughed. I tucked my head down so no one would see my blush at the innuendo.

We made a production line, with Rick spreading the sauce, Simon layering the salami, Dana piling on the mushrooms and peppers, and me sprinkling the cheese. We set two pizzas on pizza stones and put them into the oven.

We went into the living room to get the movies started, and Simon detoured to the front door. He came back with his pack slung over one shoulder.

"Can you get some glasses, Dana?" he

grinned. "I brought some red wine to go with our Italian dinner. Chianti is required for pizza."

Rick grunted. "It's supposed to be pizza and beer."

Simon swung his elbow to whack Rick in the shoulder, "You have no class. If you want to hang out with classy ladies, you have to show a bit of class! So, it is wine, you plebeian, for us, tonight." He pulled a bottle out. The bottom of it was wrapped with a straw basket.

"Ooh! The one they put the candles in!" I giggled. "How romantic!"

He smiled at me. "We have to empty it before we can put candles in it."

Dana set down four wine glasses, and Simon poured for us all. "Let's have a toast to beauty and good cooking!"

Dana and I giggled and sipped the wine. It was nasty. It left a bitter dryness on my tongue.

Simon leaned over and kissed me, his wine flavoured tongue probing for my throat.

The stove timer began to chime, and I started to pull away. Simon laughed and grabbed my hips to pull me closer. I could feel the hardness of him, and it made an unexpected tingle travel up my spine. I leaned into him, and he laughed low in his throat and murmured, "Ah, Last Chance. Do you want me as much as I want you?"

I blushed and looked away.

He gave me a final squeeze and let me go. "Go. Practise being a good wife." He chuckled and patted me on the butt as I walked away.

My heart was pounding as I arrived in the kitchen. *A good wife.*

Dana was pulling the pizzas out of the oven and lining them up on the racks on the counter.

I took a deep breath. "What can I do?"

"Get the pizza cutter. It's over there." She gestured with her chin.

I rolled it through the pizzas, slicing each into eight pieces. "These look great. Look at that, at least an inch of toppings. You're quite the chef."

She shrugged, "You all helped. It's not hard. Chance..." she broke off and grabbed my arm, "Be careful, eh?"

"I'm being careful! No blood on the pizzas." I winked at her.

"That's not what I mean." She frowned at me. "Be careful with Simon."

136

"Don't be silly. He loves..." I bit my tongue and rephrased. "He likes me. It's great." He was talking about getting married, after all. I blushed at the thought of him against me. "I'll get Simon's plate," I said. I had to practise being a wife, after all.

We passed out the plates and Simon filled the wine glasses again. The movie started. We chewed our excellent pizza and sipped the wine. The more I drank, the better it seemed to taste.

When we finished eating, Rick and Dana curled up together on a recliner and Simon settled me on top of him in another one. I nestled against his chest feeling sleepily content. He wrapped himself around me and kissed my neck. I hoped that Dana and Rick didn't notice.

I cast a furtive glance in their direction, but they were watching the movie, and keeping their eyes averted from us.

Simon burrowed his hand under my shirt and undid my bra in one smooth flick. I gasped, and he chuckled. He shifted his hips beneath me, so I could feel him beneath me.

My whole body felt electrified.

"I want you, Last Chance," he whispered. "Will you come with me?"

I pondered where he wanted me to go. Back to his town to move in with him? I didn't even know where he was from. We hadn't had any discussions at all. Our joy was more physical than that. It was elemental. I wanted it to last forever. I shifted my body, rubbing against him until he moaned.

"That's it." He rolled onto his hip and pivoted me over the arm of the chair. He stood up, bent over to scoop me off my feet, and with me giggling helplessly, he carried me over his shoulder into Dana's guest room. He shut the door behind us and tossed me onto the bed. I bounced a bit, and then sat up. He pulled me to him, kissing me until my head was spinning. He reached out for the bottom of my shirt, lifting it off smoothly. I raised my arms and was standing in front of him with my undone bra hanging pointlessly in front of me. Heat flooded through me, and I wanted him. Badly. I pulled his shirt off. He groaned.

We fell onto the bed, and I thought, *this is really happening. I'm going to lose my virginity to the most handsome guy I've ever met.* Suddenly another thought hit me, and I gasped, "Wait! Do you have a condom?"

"Shit. No." He scowled for a minute.

I stared at him.

He looked at me as he panted slightly. Finally he shook his head. "I know what to do. I'll just pull out before I finish. It'll be all right. You won't get pregnant."

"I don't think..." I started to argue, but then his mouth was on me, and I couldn't think of anything but how much my body wanted his.

13

"Chancey?" Dana knocked on the bedroom door. "Are you awake?"

"I am now," I mumbled, I looked around trying to figure out where I was. As the night before came rushing back, I turned to say good morning to Simon, but he wasn't there. My heart constricted. "When did the guys leave?" I called to Dana.

"After midnight. One or two o'clock. I don't know."

"Oh." I fought my way out of tangled blankets and reached for my jeans.

"Are you okay?"

"You can come in," I said, as I pulled on my bra.

Dana opened the door and just looked

at me with a concerned expression.

"Why wouldn't I be okay?" I smiled at her. Simon and I had a great night, after all.

She shrugged. "He didn't hurt you?"

I laughed. "No, of course not." Truth be told, I did feel sore, but I wasn't going to complain. Simon loved me, and there would be many more nights when we fell into each other's arms and enjoyed each other's bodies. Suddenly I was ravenous. "What's for breakfast?"

She laughed then, shaking her head. "I've got waffle batter proofing. There's fruit, whipped cream, and fancy fruit syrups."

"When did you get to be such a good cook? Are you practising for marrying Rick?"

"Are you crazy? Why would you even think about marriage? We're way too young."

"Living together, then."

She just rolled her eyes. "I doubt I'll be with Rick that long. How many teen couples end up in long term relationships? Seriously."

"Simon and I will be."

She wrinkled her forehead as she raised her brows. "Chancey..."

"Stop Dana. I know we will be. He loves me. You'd know if you... Never mind. Just trust me. We will be together for a long time."

"Come make waffles."

So I did. They were tasty. I couldn't help talking about Simon while we cooked,

143

about how handsome he was, how gorgeous his body was, how amazing it was when he kissed me.

As she was doing the dishes afterwards, Dana rolled her eyes. "I get it. You're in love."

"Yup," I sighed, folding my arms on the table and resting my head on them. "I'm in love with the most perfect man on the planet."

"I hope you're right."

"What does that mean?"

She shrugged. "I don't know. Something bothers me about him. He seems too slick."

"You're just jealous."

"You know I'm not, Chancey. Rick is gorgeous, too. I'm glad you're in love. I just wish I felt like we can trust Simon."

"Has Rick said anything?"

"Not really. But there's a secret reason why he's staying with them. He says he can't tell me."

"I don't believe it," I said, standing up. "I've got to go. Talk to you later." I didn't want to hear anything bad about Simon.

I went home feeling annoyed at Dana. I kept checking my phone for texts. None came from Simon, so I wrote Dana instead.

"I DON'T KNOW WHAT'S WRONG!" I texted to her. "DO YOU THINK HE'S SICK?"

"DON'T SEND HIM A MILLION TEXTS," she replied. "YOU DON'T WANT HIM TO THINK YOU'RE NEEDY."

"I AM! I NEED HIM!" But I held off sending any more texts until about midnight. I'd been trying to sleep, but I was thrashing around, my head full of worries.

Finally, I gave in and texted him a simple, "HOW WAS YOUR DAY?"

He didn't write back.

The next day, I wrote "MISS YOU."

He didn't write back. Was he ghosting me?

After three days, I texted Rick. "WHAT'S UP WITH SIMON?"

He wrote back, "HE'S GONE HOME."

My stomach dropped into my knees. I swallowed a nauseous feeling. "WHAT DO YOU MEAN BY HOME?"

"I MEAN HE LEFT. HE ISN'T HERE ANYMORE."

"HE'S NOT ANSWERING ME. WHAT'S WRONG WITH HIS PHONE?"

"I'M CALLING YOU," Rick replied, and in a moment my phone rang.

Even though I knew it was Rick, I couldn't help the way my heart leapt in the hope that it was Simon. "Hey."

"Look, Chancey. Simon is gone. He isn't coming back, and he won't text you or talk to you."

"Why not?" That didn't make any sense.

"Don't be mad. He told me that once he's slept with his current project, he is done with her. He never sleeps with any of them twice."

"Project?" I choked. "What project?"

 "You. You were his project. He's done now. He said to tell you that you made his holiday really fun."

"Fun?" I said weakly.

"Chancey, he's on probation. He's a minor, so my parents weren't allowed to say anything about why he was here. I don't know the details, but there was a girl who didn't say yes to him. You know what I

147

mean? It turns out he's not allowed to be around girls under sixteen."

"Like me." I whispered.

"Yeah. When my parents found out he'd been seeing you, they reported it to his probation officer. That's why he's gone. He can't text you. He's not allowed to be in contact with you."

I wanted to puke. "Right. Thanks for telling me. Wish you'd thought about telling before."

"I hinted as much as I was allowed. Dana did, too. I didn't know all the conditions then. I only know because I overheard them shouting at Simon. I wish I could have told you more from the beginning. Warned out properly. You couldn't accept what we could tell you."

Tears burned in my eyes. Had they

tried? I tried to remember. I hadn't heard them if they had. "Yeah. Right," I muttered, trying not to let him hear my tears. "Talk to you later."

I hung up and stared blindly at the TV as I let the tears fall.

So much for my romantic adventure.

14

The weeks went by and I did my best to forget about Simon.

When Mom wondered why I was looking sad, I told her I had done badly on a math test.

Brian asked what had happened to 'that guy you were seeing,' but at my expression he just nodded thoughtfully. He hadn't asked again.

Mom had her period again and spent another week in tears.

Life went on. A couple of months passed.

I woke in the middle of the night with a turbulent growling in my stomach. I lay there, blinking into the night, absorbing the sensation. Suddenly, my stomach heaved, and I thrust the blankets off me and rushed into the bathroom. I threw up my dinner, rinsed my mouth, and then brushed my teeth.

"Chancey?" Brian asked, tapping lightly on the bathroom door, "Are you okay?"

"Yeah, I'm fine. My stomach was just upset. I feel all right now." I opened the door and smiled at him. "I'm heading back to bed. Sorry for disturbing you."

"You're sure you're all right?"

I nodded and shut my bedroom door. I heard him rattling around in the kitchen. I rolled over onto my stomach and shifted uncomfortably, my chest hurt, as if my period was coming. I finally had to sleep on my side.

In the morning, I woke to the smell of

bacon. I love bacon, but today it made my stomach churn. I found myself gagging again. I barely made it to the bathroom in time.

"Honey?" said Mom. "Are you throwing up in there?"

"Yeah. I must have the flu."

"Breakfast is ready. Pancakes, eggs, and bacon."

I opened the door and sniffed. "The bacon smells gross."

"You love the smell of bacon," she said, narrowing her eyes.

I wrinkled my nose. "Not today. It makes me want to throw up."

Brian came out of their room. Mom looked at him. "Did you hear that?"

He nodded. "She was up last night, too."

"I'm sorry I woke you! I can't help that I

have the flu."

"I hope so," Brian said.

Mom tightened her lips.

"What? What's wrong?"

"Nothing, hon. Why don't you go back to bed, if you're not feeling well. I can bring you some pancakes in bed, if you like."

"No, I'll go change and meet you at the table. It's hard eating in bed."

I brushed my teeth. The toothpaste made me gag. I felt strange. Not achy, gross, and really sick like I usually did when I had the flu. My head was fine. It was just my stomach that seemed ridiculously sensitive. And my tender chest. I pulled back my lips to study my teeth in the mirror. I looked really good, too. I didn't look sick. My hair was shiny, and my complexion had cleared up. No zits were in evidence for once.

I pulled on my yoga pants and a t-shirt, humming to myself.

"It's not possible," my mother hissed at Brian, down in the kitchen. "She's a good girl!"

"Of course, it's possible. She had a boyfriend, Megan. All it takes is a boy."

I scowled in the mirror as I headed out into the hall.

"Why are you talking about boyfriends? Simon and I broke up. He's far away. Don't worry." I said as I flopped into my chair.

Not that we'd ever really been going out, except in my vivid imagination.

It sucked that he wasn't a very good boyfriend after all, but I had to say that I'd had an adventure or two because of him. I could thank him for that, at least.

I sat down at the table and reached out my fork to stab a few pancakes.

"What happened with Simon, Hon?" Mom asked. "Did he do something to make you want to break up with him?"

"Nothing exciting. He had to go back home." They were looking at me with sad puppy eyes, like I was pathetic. "It's okay," I added, trying to look nonchalant. "We decided that a long-distance relationship was not likely to work out, and it was better to break up, that's all."

Brian nodded sagely, "Very mature of you."

I chewed my pancakes and didn't meet their eyes.

"Chancey, I don't want to make any

insinuations..." Brian began.

"Brian..." Mom interrupted.

He shrugged, "We have to ask, Megan."

"Ask what?" I said, munching on a mouthful of pancake.

Brian took a deep breath and blurted out, "Is there any chance that you could be suffering from morning sickness?"

"But you only get morning sickness if you're pregnant," I said.

He just looked at me.

I looked over at Mom. She was staring at her plate and biting her lip.

"I can't be pregnant."

"Because you haven't had sex, right?" said Mom.

My cheeks flamed. "No, because he..." I swallowed and looked out the window. "He pulled out before he..." I swallowed again.

156

"You know."

"Oh, God," said Mom, staring at me with incredibly wide eyes.

Brian nodded. "Tell us that you used a condom."

I blushed again and studied my plate.

"Right. We're making a doctor's appointment for you to take a pregnancy test."

"I really don't think that's necessary," I argued. "I'm not pregnant. I mean, it was only the one time."

"When was your last period?" Mom asked, setting her hand on my arm.

I visualized my calendar and the little check mark that I usually made in the first week of the month. I realized hadn't made a check mark this month and it was almost over. My eyes must have answered the question, because she nodded. "You're having a test."

15

"The doctor phoned," Mom said, as I walked into the kitchen after school. "She wants to see you. I made an appointment for you tomorrow after school. I'll pick you up."

"Did she say why she wants to see me?" Good news or bad news, I meant. I opened the fridge to get the milk.

Mom shook her head. "She didn't."

I poured the milk into my favourite Tweety Bird mug. "It doesn't seem like it'd be worth her time to call me in to tell me that I'm not pregnant, though. Does it?"

"Yeah. I was thinking the same thing."

I sipped the milk thoughtfully and sighed. I was pregnant. What was I going to do?

"Chancey?"

I looked over my mug. Mom's eyes were big and shiny, like she was about to cry. They were plaintive eyes, like I used when I wanted them to extend my curfew or buy me a new pair of jeans when I'd already used up my allowance. I got a funny feeling in my stomach. "What?"

"If you are pregnant, everything will be fine. You'll stay in school, have the baby, and I'll, I mean, we'll raise her." She stared earnestly at me. "It doesn't have to change anything for you. It will be okay."

I looked down at my belly, still flat. It was hard to believe that there could be a person growing in there. It was kind of gross to imagine, actually. Some little alien bean had lodged in my uterus and I was

going to have to push it out my privates
when it was the size of a basketball.
Ouch. That would not be fun.

I looked back at Mom's hopeful eyes.
"Her? You think it's a girl?"

She shrugged. "Or him."

"What does Brian say?"

"He's fine with it."

I nodded. Of course, he'd be fine with it.
It was the perfect solution for them. Mom
got her baby at last. Brian wouldn't have
to listen to her crying every month. This
was great for her. Was it great for me?
"I'm going to get started on my
homework," I said, rinsing the glass and
setting it into the dishwasher.

I shut the bedroom door and flopped
onto my bed.

I'd been so blind. I had been completely

taken in by Simon's good looks. I had been overwhelmed by the chemistry between us, and I hadn't bothered to get to know the not-so-great guy under his skin.

I had been so keen for a romantic adventure; I'd missed the part about having an actual positive relationship with someone. I still didn't even know where he lived, let alone how old he was, or what his favourite band was. I had imagined a perfect life with someone who didn't exist.

I knew more about the characters in my silent reading book at school.

Delia had been right, that warm night in Laketon outside the Purple Barn when she'd warned that he was trouble. Would I have a story to tell her next summer!

Simon hadn't been interested in the real me, either. A month of going out with him, and he'd never figured out that I was the girl he'd danced with at The Purple Barn.

I had made a terrible mistake trusting he was what I imagined he was despite all the warnings. Now I might have to face the consequences of that mistake every day over breakfast. Some little Simon faced person could blink up at me and call me Mom. Me.

The very idea of it made my stomach heave again, and I sprinted for the bathroom. This little person was taking after its father already. I was always nauseous around Simon, too.

Mom knocked on the bathroom door. "Chancey? Are you okay?"

"Yeah," I said, flushing the toilet and washing my hands. I brushed my teeth. I could feel her hovering outside the door. "Mom, it's okay. I'm not scraping out my innards with a shaver or anything."

"Chancey!" she squawked. "How can you say such a thing!"

I opened the door and met her eyes. "It was a joke. If I don't joke, I will cry. Would you prefer tears?"

She blinked. Tears were her preferred method of dealing with trauma relating to babies. Maybe she'd never considered that there were other alternatives. She cleared her throat. "Chancey, it will all be fine. I promise. You can make whatever decision you need to make, and we'll support you, but know that we love you, and we will love your baby. Our baby. If you want to continue your pregnancy."

I looked into her eyes and understood

that a stupid mistake can sometimes bring happiness with it. Simon had given us a weird gift.

It wasn't something I would have wanted, but I had wanted to have sex with him. I'd been willing to risk sex without birth control.

That was dumb.

But.

It would be okay. I had learned some hard lessons in the last couple of months, and I was never going to be able to forget them. There'd be a walking talking reminder in a few months.

There was definitely enough love in this house to share, though. I wrapped my arms around her and hugged her tightly. "Thanks, Mom."

HERE IS A SNEAK PEEK AT THE NEXT
LIFE IN LAKETON BOOK:

Wildfire!

"Come on Zuzu!" I called. "Jump! Jump! Jump!" I ran along the row of dog jumps I'd set up on the dried brown grass of our front yard.

Zuzu, my white standard poodle, ran along behind me, tongue lolling out of her mouth, completely ignoring the jumps. She pulled ahead and stopped short right in front of me, eyes twinkling.

I stumbled, trying not to stop but tumbled over her and collapsed onto the grass, which stuck to my sweaty shirt.

Zuzu wagged her tail and covered me with kisses.

"Oh, Zuzu!" I laughed, rubbing her curly white coat and soft silky ears as I tried to twist away from her tongue. "You win. It's much too hot for this."

My brother Brian pulled up in his pick-up. His red Wildfire Service shirt was filthy, as were his black pants. He looked over to me as he pulled his duffle bag out of the truck. box "That's disgusting, Delia. You're never going to find a boy who wants to kiss you if you let your dog do that."

I was about to argue that I wasn't looking for a boy to kiss, when the screen door opened, and our mom threw her arms wide.

"The prodigal returns!" Our mom threw her arms wide open for a hug. "How's fire fighting?" She beamed at him proudly.

"It's okay. My crew has a day off since our fire is under control. The mop-up crew is going in now."

Mom looked over at me and scowled, "Get

167

off the lawn, young lady! The neighbours will think we're raising a little hooligan instead of a girl! Go put on a dress and come help me with dinner while your brother has a shower." She turned away from me and wrapped an arm around Brian. "Leave your dirty clothes outside the bathroom door and Delia can put them in the laundry for you." She looked up at the sky and glanced over her shoulder at the dark grey clouds gathering over the hills. "Looks like rain at last. You'd better put away those dog things."

I scowled back at her, but she didn't see me, since she'd already followed Brian into the house. That was fine. I was in no rush to put on a stupid dress and do chores my stupid brother was perfectly capable of doing for himself. Why couldn't he take his own clothes down to the laundry room and put them into the washing machine?

Zuzu nudged my elbow. "I know, girl, I

know." I could imagine my father's serious voice: 'There are pink jobs and blue jobs. Be proud of who you are!' I pulled myself up and went to gather the jumps. As I approached each frame, Zuzu leapt over it like a deer, just to show me she could jump if she felt like it. She glanced back at me with mischief in her eyes as she landed. "You're a brat," I told her, as she bounded over the next jump before I could get to it.

"Your dog doesn't look very smart. That hair cut is ridiculous."

I looked up to see Chris Turlock from school standing at the road.

"She's probably smarter than you. Her hair cut is five hundred years old, created to protect poodles while they're retrieving game from water. It's a hunting hair cut."

Chris just rolled his eyes. "Yeah, right."

I wasn't going to argue with him. Show poodles have super big hair; Zuzu's is much shorter, in the original ancient style. Shaved bare on the back legs to allow for swimming, but with longer hair for protection over the chest, ankle joints and kidneys. I thought it was gorgeous.

Chris watched Zuzu prancing circles around me before he shrugged and came up the sidewalk toward me. "That's Brian's truck, right? Is he home?"

Zuzu stepped between us and stared at him.

He took another step forward.

Zuzu growled. Her whole body was tense

"Whoa there!" He put out his arms, ready to defend himself if she leapt at him. "I'm not going to hurt anybody!"

"How does she know that after all those insults?" I set a hand on my hip and glared at him. I ran my other hand down Zuzu's back. "Good girl."

In the distance there was a rumble of

thunder.

Chris took a step back. "I just wanted to see how things are going with Brian."

"He's just gotten back home. He's taking a shower and then he has to have family dinner. You know how my mother is. She needs to gaze adoringly at her favourite child who is risking life and limb to protect the forests. Do you want me to give him a message?"

"Just tell him I'm on the Volunteer Fire Department now. We're training tonight if he wants to come over and give us any tips."

Brian was working for the Wildfire Service this summer. He'd started as a junior firefighter with the Laketon Volunteer Fire Department when he was fifteen. That gave him training and experience that got him on the Wildfire Service when he was nineteen. It was a dangerous job, but it paid well. I wanted to do it, too, but my parents said it was a 'blue job.'

"I'll tell him." I said, turning away and hoisting the frames onto my shoulder.

"Do you want some help carrying those jumps?"

"Why? Do I look like I need help?"

"Don't be so touchy! I just thought I'd be nice!" Huge drops of rain began spattering on the ground around us in big drops that bounced on the sidewalk pavement and caused puffs of dust where they landed on the dry ground. We hadn't had rain in weeks.

"I'm perfectly capable," I said, hefting three jumps onto my shoulder. "Go to your training. You don't want to be late."

"You know, if you were nicer, you might have a better chance of attracting a boyfriend."

What was it with people thinking I needed a boyfriend? I let out an exasperated sigh and spun on my heels. "Come on, Zuzu."

I side-stepped my way past the raised

garden beds that filled the back yard and stacked the jumps against the shed, before I walked back to shut the gate. Zuzu was a good girl, but like most standard poodles, she had a mind of her own. If she felt like visiting Horace the Pug or Daisy the Labrador down the street, she'd be out of the yard. She stood waist high to me and was agile enough to climb any fence, so both our five feet of backyard fence and the gate were really just suggestions. Thankfully, most of the time she just wanted to be with me, and both sufficed.

We didn't have an animal control officer in Laketon, and everyone knew Zuzu belonged to me. Still, I didn't want to see her running loose, where she might get hit by a car or picked up by a tourist who didn't know she had a home.

"Delia!" Mom shouted out the window, "quit fooling with that dog and get in here! We have work to do." She dropped her voice and muttered, "We never should have let you have that puppy."

I smirked. That had been Mom's constant refrain since I'd saved my money from a summer working at Maggie's Shake Shack to buy a purebred standard poodle from performance lines. I wanted a smart dog to train for agility and obedience and I got one. Sometimes I was afraid Zuzu might be training me more than I was training her, but she was my baby and she made me happy.

The rain was pouring down now, so my hair was plastered to my head and Zuzu looked like a wet mop. The longer hair on her head, neck, and back curled up from the moisture.

We stood under the covered deck, and Zuzu shook herself dry, spraying me down. I ruffled her ears and kissed the top of her head. "You're a good girl, Zuzu."

As the backdoor slammed behind us, there was a flash of lightning. Automatically, I began to count under my breath: one thousand, two thousand, three thousand, and then a rumble. The storm wasn't far off.

I walked down the hall and gathered up the pile of clothes Brian had left outside the bathroom, then went downstairs to put them in the washer. When I came back up, Zuzu was turning circles in her basket. She flopped down inelegantly in a tight ball. Brian was in the living room, now wearing his old Laketon High shorts.

Another flash of lightning lit the sky. "I don't like that," he said as the thunder rumbled. "It's so dry out there. Every flash is going to cause a fire that my colleagues are going to have deal with."

Mom bustled in, "We'll just pray that the rain immediately douses any fire started by lightning," she said. "Delia, I thought I told you to get changed for dinner? Did you put Brian's laundry in?"

175

"Of course." I bit back the urge to roll my eyes. "Can't you hear the washing machine?"

She tilted her head. "Ah. Good. Thank you. Go get dressed."

There was another flash. Brian opened the front door and sniffed. "Does anyone else smell smoke?"

ABOUT THE AUTHOR

Shawn L. Bird (BA, MEd) is a high school English teacher, an author, and a poet in the beautiful Shuswap region of British Columbia. She is the author of over twenty publications for both teens and adults, including short stories, poetry, novellas, and novels.

In her spare time, she hangs out with her husband, annoys her kids, trains her talented miniature poodle in tricks and agility, plays the harp, and serves her community with Shuswap Rotary Club, all while wearing truly awesome shoes.

Visit her website at www.shawnbird.com to learn more about her books. Sign up for her newsletter for updates about new publications.

Shawn is happy to visit high school classes to discuss reading, writing, or Life in Laketon, either virtually or in person.

You're invited to write to Shawn at

Lintusen Press

PO Box 10019

Salmon Arm BC

Canada V1E 3B9

or

Shawn@ShawnBird.com

WATCH FOR MORE BOOKS ABOUT

LIFE IN LAKETON:

1. Back at You

2. After #8

3. Chancey

4. Wildfire!

5. While I Was Out